W9-AGZ-778

# Junie B. Jones
## Smells Something Fishy

by Barbara Park

illustrated by Denise Brunkus

A STEPPING STONE BOOK™

Random House 🏠 New York

*My sincere thanks to my editor,*
*Michelle Knudsen, for her insight, patience,*
*and (best of all) her* splendiferous *sense of humor!*
*Junie B. and I couldn't be in better hands.*

Text copyright © 1998 by Barbara Park
Illustrations copyright © 1998 by Denise Brunkus
All rights reserved under International and Pan-American Copyright
Conventions. Published in the United States by Random House, Inc., and
simultaneously in Canada by Random House of Canada Limited, Toronto.

www.randomhouse.com/kids

*Library of Congress Cataloging-in-Publication Data*
Park, Barbara. Junie B. Jones smells something fishy / by Barbara Park ;
illustrated by Denise Brunkus.
p.  cm. —  "A Stepping Stone book."
SUMMARY: Frustrated because the rules for her class's Pet Day will not let
her take her dog to school, Junie B. Jones considers taking a raccoon, a
worm, a dead fish, and other unusual replacements.
ISBN 0-679-89130-7 (pbk.) — ISBN 0-679-99130-1 (lib. bdg.)  [1. Pets—
Fiction.   2. Kindergarten—Fiction.
3. Schools—Fiction.]  I. Brunkus, Denise, ill. II. Title.
PZ7.P2197Jty  1998  [Fic]—dc21  98-28176

Printed in the United States of America  20 19 18 17 16 15 14 13 12
A STEPPING STONE BOOK is a trademark of Random House, Inc.

# Contents

# 1/ Pet Day

My name is Junie B. Jones. The B stands for Beatrice. Except I don't like Beatrice. I just like B and that's all.

And guess what else?

B rhymes with P. And P stands for pet. And pet reminds me of what happened at my school today.

First, I was sitting at my table doing my work.

Then all of a sudden, my teacher stood up. And she clapped her loud hands together.

Her name is Mrs. She has another name, too. But I just like Mrs. and that's all.

"Boys and girls! May I have your attention, please?" she said. "I've got some very exciting news. Next week is National Pet Week. And to help celebrate our wonderful pets, Room Nine is going to have Pet Day!"

I springed up from my chair real thrilled.

"HURRAY, PEOPLE! HURRAY! HURRAY! WE'RE GOING TO HAVE PET DAY!" I shouted.

My feet skipped all around the room. 'Cause they wanted to spread the news, that's why!

"PET DAY! WE'RE GOING TO HAVE PET DAY, CHARLOTTE!" I hollered.

"PET DAY! WE'RE GOING TO HAVE PET DAY, JAMAL!"

"PET DAY! WE'RE GOING TO HAVE

PET DAY, YOU MEANIE JIM I HATE!"

Just then, Mrs. grabbed me by my s'penders.

S'penders is the grownup word for the *straps that hold your pants up*.

I looked around very worried.

"Yeah, only here's the problem," I said. "If you pull off the s'penders—boom—the pants fall down."

Mrs. did a frown at me.

"Sit…down…right…*now,*" she said real scary.

I did a gulp.

"Will do," I said.

Then I hurried up back to my seat. And Mrs. went to the front of the room again.

She told us all the rules about Pet Day.

She said that Pet Day will be next Monday. And if you have a cat or a dog, you can bring in his picture. And Mrs. will hang it on the bulletin board.

"But please, boys and girls...no cats or dogs at school, okay?" she said. "The only animals you can bring to school are pets in cages."

I springed up again.

"Whew! That was a close one!" I said. "'Cause I have a dog named Tickle! And at first, I thought I could only bring in his picture. But now I will bring him in a dog cage!"

Mrs. shook her head.

"No, Junie B. I'm afraid you didn't understand. No dogs or cats will be allowed at school at *all*. Not even if you bring them in cages. I'm going to decorate a special bulletin board for all the dog and cat pictures."

I hanged my head real disappointed.

4

"Shoot," I said.

'Cause a dog picture isn't even fun, that's why.

Just then, my bestest friend named Grace waved her hand in the air.

"Can I bring my goldfish, Slicky?" she asked. "Is a fishbowl the same thing as a cage?"

Mrs. smiled.

"Yes, Grace. A goldfish will be just fine."

After that, my other bestest friend named Lucille raised her hand, too.

"Teacher! Guess what I'm going to bring? I'm going to bring a picture of my new pony! And also I am going to wear my expensive new riding outfit! That way, everyone will see how cute I look when I ride!"

Mrs. stared at Lucille a real long time.

"What a treat that will be," she said finally.

Lucille poked me with her finger.

"I can't wait for Pet Day! Can you, Junie B.? Just wait till you see how cute I look in my riding boots!" she said.

I didn't say anything back.

She poked me again.

"Pet Day is going to be fun! Don't you think? Huh, Junie B.? Don't you think Pet Day will be fun? Don't you? Don't you?"

Just then, I leaned real close to her face.

"Do not poke me one more time, and I *mean* it," I grouched. "What is so fun about bringing a dog picture? Huh, Lucille? What is so fun about that? Huh? Huh? Huh?"

After that, I put my head on the table.

And I covered up with my arms.

And I didn't come out till the end of school.

# 2/
## The Secret
## About Twitter

Me and that Grace rode the bus home together.

I did not speak to that girl.

'Cause she kept on being happy about Slicky. And so what kind of crummy attitude is that?

I walked in my house real glum.

Grandma Helen Miller was babysitting my baby brother named Ollie.

"Uh-oh. It looks like someone had a bad day at school," she said.

I raised my hand very weakish.

"Me, Grandma. It was me. I am the one who had the bad day."

After that, I gave her a paper from my teacher. It was the rules about Pet Day.

Grandma Miller put Ollie in his swing.

Then me and her sat on the couch. And I waited while she read the paper.

"Oh dear," she said. "You can't take Tickle, can you?"

I shook my head real gloomy.

"Not even in a cage," I said.

I did a sad sigh. "Where's the justice here, Helen?" I asked.

Grandma smiled very understanding.

Then she gave me a hug.

And she said don't call her Helen.

"I don't know what to tell you, sweetie," she said. "Unless you get another pet before Pet Day, I guess you're just going to have to accept this."

My eyes started to cry a teeny bit.

"But Mother and Daddy won't buy me another pet, Grandma. 'Cause I already asked for a bunny and a goat and a bat and a rat. But they keep on saying no, no, no, no."

Grandma read the rules again.

"Wait a second here," she said. "Why didn't I see this before? It says you can bring a bird."

I shrugged my shoulders. "Yeah? So?"

"So you can take my *canary!*" she said. "I'll let you take Twitter!"

I looked and looked at that woman.

Then I patted her hand very nice.

And I whispered a secret in her ear.

"Yeah, only here's the problem. I hate that dumb bird," I said.

Grandma Miller looked surprised.

"You *hate* him? You hate Twitter?" she asked.

I showed her my finger.

"He pecked me, Grandma. He pecked my finger, remember that? And I didn't even do anything to that guy."

Grandma Miller made squinty eyes at me.

"You put a potato on his head," she said. "I would have pecked you, too."

I smiled kind of nervous.

"It was a hat," I said real soft.

After that, me and Grandma Miller sat there kind of stiffish. And we didn't talk for lots of minutes.

Finally, I tapped on her.

"Do you have any other pets at your house?" I asked. "Any pets I'm not aware of?"

Grandma Miller laughed a little bit.

"Not unless we catch that crazy old raccoon that keeps breaking into our garbage can every night," she said.

Then she laughed some more.

And guess what?

I laughed, too!

'Cause that woman is a genius, I tell you!

# 3/ The Boss

On Saturday, I got out of bed very thrilled.

Then I runned to the garage.

And I grabbed my daddy's fishing net.

And I zoomed right into the kitchen.

Mother was eating cereal.

"Mother! Mother! Guess why I have this fishing net! Guess, Mother! Guess! Guess!"

I couldn't wait for her to guess.

"'CAUSE TODAY'S THE DAY I'M CATCHING THAT CRAZY OLD RAC-COON!" I shouted.

14

Mother closed her eyes.

"No, Junie B. No. We already talked about this, remember? We discussed the raccoon at dinner last night."

I smiled very happy.

"I already know that! I already know we discussed the raccoon!"

Mother looked confused.

"But Daddy and I said *no,* Junie B.," she said. "We said you could *not* catch a raccoon. Raccoons have sharp claws and teeth, remember?"

"Yes! Of course I remember! That's how come I got this net, Mother! See how long the handle is? Now I will be safe from him!"

Mother spelled the word no.

"N-o...no," she said.

I stamped my foot.

"Y-e-s...yes," I said back. "I *have* to,

Mother. I have to catch a raccoon for Pet Day. Grandma Miller even *said* I could. And she is the boss of you."

Just then, a miracle happened.

And it is called *my Grandma Helen Miller walked right in my back door!*

Mother looked up.

"Oh look. It's the boss of me," she said kind of grouchy.

I runned at my grandma very happy.

"Grandma Miller! Grandma Miller! I am so glad to see you! 'Cause Mother said I can't catch a raccoon! And so now you have to make her!"

I stood back to give her room.

"Okay. Go," I said.

Then I waited and waited. But Grandma didn't do anything.

"Okay! Go!" I said louder.

Only just then, I saw something that made me even happier!

And it's called *my grandma was wearing her fishing hat!*

My eyes popped out at that thing.

"Grandma! Hey, Grandma! You're wearing your fishing hat! And so that must mean you're going to the lake today!"

I quick ran to the front door.

"Is Grampa Miller going to the lake with you? Is he out there in the truck?"

I looked outside.

"HEY! HE IS, GRANDMA! HE *IS* OUT THERE IN THE TRUCK!"

I opened the door.

"GRAMPA MILLER! HEY, GRAMPA FRANK MILLER! GOOD NEWS! I CAN COME TO THE LAKE WITH YOU, I BELIEVE! 'CAUSE THERE'S LOTS OF

RACCOONS TO CATCH UP THERE!
EVEN MORE THAN AT YOUR HOUSE,
PROBABLY!"

I zoomed back to the kitchen.

"Here, Grandma! Hold my raccoon net! I will put on my clothes and be back in a jiffy."

Jiffy is the nickname for speedy quick.

Grandma Miller grabbed me by my p.j.'s.

"No, honey. Wait," she said. "I'm afraid you can't come with us today. We're meeting some friends, and we're already late. We just stopped by to borrow your daddy's ice chest."

Just then, I felt very crumbling inside.

"Yeah, only I *have* to come, Grandma. I have to," I said. "Or else how will I catch a raccoon today?"

Grandma Miller bended down next to me.

"Yes, well, you see…that's another thing, sweetie," she said. "About the raccoon…I was just *kidding* when I said that, Junie B.

I never dreamed you would take me seriously."

Just then, my nose started to sniffle.

"Yeah, well, you dreamed wrong, Helen," I said.

Grandma Miller hugged me real tight.

"Oh, come on now. Don't cry," she said. "There are lots of other animals you can catch for Pet Day. Animals that are *much* nicer than raccoons."

I shook my head real fast.

"No, there are not, either, Grandma Miller. You are just saying that to trick me," I said.

Then I stood there and stood there a real long time.

'Cause what if she *wasn't* tricking? What if there really *was* lots of other animals?

Finally, I did a big breath. "Okay. Tell me

the other animals. But this better be good."

Grandma Miller did a smile.

"Wait right here," she said.

Then she ran out to her truck and back again.

She was hiding something behind her back.

"Junie B., I've got someone who would love to meet you," she said. "Close your eyes. And I'll put him in your hand."

My tummy got butterflies in it.

"What is it, Grandma? Will it tickle me? Will I like it? It won't bite me, will it, Grandma Miller? Huh? It won't, right?"

Then I closed my eyes real tight.

And my grandma opened up my fingers.

And she put the surprise right in my hand.

# 4/ Ooey Gooey

"EEEW! YUCK! IT'S A WORM! IT'S A WORM! GET IT OFF ME, GRANDMA! GET IT OFF RIGHT NOW!" I yelled.

Grandma Miller quick took back the worm.

"For heaven's sake, Junie B. What in the world is the matter with you? It's just a baby earthworm. Look how teeny he is. This little fellow would make a *wonderful* pet."

I did a huffy breath at her.

"Yeah, only worms cannot be pets,

Grandma. 'Cause pets have fur so you can *pet* them. And worms just have ooey gooey skin."

Grandma Miller looked surprised at me.

"Don't be silly," she said. "Not all pets have fur. My bird Twitter doesn't have fur, and he's a pet. And goldfish don't have fur. And hermit crabs don't have fur. And lizards don't have fur. And—"

I covered my ears with my hands.

"Okay, okay. Enough with the fur," I said. "But worms don't have eyes or ears, either. And they don't have legs or tails or feet or necks. And they don't chirp or bark or cluck or meow. And so what kind of stupid pet do you call that?"

Grandma Miller thought and thought.

Then she smiled real big.

"I'd call that the kind of pet that won't

wake up the neighbors or sniff the company or scratch himself silly," she said back.

After that, she stood up. And she gave the baby earthworm to Mother.

"I'll leave this little guy with your mother for now," she said. "You can think it over and see if you want to keep him. I'll check back with you later."

Then she kissed me on my head.

And she grabbed the ice chest.

And she hurried out the door.

Mother looked at the baby worm in her hand. "My goodness. You *are* a little one, aren't you?" she said.

She got an empty mayonnaise jar out of the cabinet.

Then she poked holes in the lid for air. And she put the baby worm inside.

Mother looked at him in there.

"You don't even know where you are, do you, little fella?" she said. "I bet it's kind of scary in there all by yourself."

I turned my back on her. 'Cause I knew what she was up to, that's why.

"You can't make me like him, Mother," I said. "Nobody can make me like him."

"Of course not," said Mother. "But just because *you* don't like him doesn't mean *I* can't like him."

She talked to the worm some more.

"Hmm. Maybe you'd be happier if you had some dirt to crawl around in," she said. "Let's go outside and see what we can do."

After that, Mother put on her jacket. And she went outside. And she digged in the dirt from her garden.

She came inside and showed me the jar.

It looked kind of cute in there.

There was a rock and a stick and a dan-
delion and some clovers.

I peeked at the baby worm.

He peeked back, I think.

"Yeah, only I still don't like him," I said kind of softer.

I rocked back and forth on my feet.

"And anyway...even if I *did* like him, I don't know what worms eat. And so what would I even feed that guy?"

Mother ruffled my hair.

"Are you kidding? That's the best part about worms," she said. "They get all of their food right from the soil. You don't have to feed them anything at all."

Just then, my baby brother started to cry.

"Uh-oh. The baby's crying," she said. "Here. Take this."

Then she quick handed me the jar.

And she runned right out of the room.

# 5/ Catching Friends

I watched the little worm very careful.

He wiggled himself into the dirt.

I tapped on the glass.

"Yeah, only here's the problem. Now I can't see you anymore. And so what fun is that?" I asked.

I took off the lid and put my lips in the jar.

"Come out, come out, wherever you are!" I said real loud.

Then I waited very patient. But the worm did not come out.

"Hey, in there! Don't you even know I'm talking to you?"

Then—all of a sudden—my brain thought of something very important!

Of *course* he didn't know I was talking to him!

How could he know I was talking to him if he didn't even have a name!

I quick closed my eyes real tight. And I tried to think of a worm name.

Pretty soon, my eyes springed wide open.

"NOODLE!" I said real thrilled. "I will name you Noodle! 'Cause noodles and worms are twins, practically!"

I yelled in the jar again.

"HERE, NOODLE! HERE, NOODLEY LITTLE NOODLE!"

Just then, Mother peeked her head in the kitchen door.

"What's all the shouting about in here?" she asked. "Who's Noodle?"

I pointed to my dirt jar.

"Noodle is my worm," I said. "Only he crawled way into the dirt. And now he won't come out. Not even when I call his name."

Mother looked in the jar.

"Hmm...maybe he's taking a nap," she said. "Or maybe he's just exploring his new home."

I tapped on my chin.

"Maybe," I said. "Or maybe he might be looking for some friends to play with."

Just then, I did a gasp.

"Mother! Mother! I bet that's it! I bet little Noodle is lonely in there!

31

I bet he's looking for friends!"

I zoomed to the closet speedy fast. And I put on my sweater.

"HOLD ON, LITTLE NOODLE! HOLD ON! HOLD ON! 'CAUSE I CAN HELP YOU WITH THIS PROBLEM, I THINK!"

After that, I grabbed Noodle's jar.

And me and him zoomed outside to the garden again.


Friends do not come easy.

First, I tried to catch a butterfly. But it quick flied away.

Then I tried to catch a grasshopper. But it wouldn't stand still.

Also I tried to catch a cricket and a gnat and a lizard. But those guys would not cooperate, either.

Finally, I sat down in the grass real glum.

"I am a flop at this job," I said.

Only just then, I saw something very wonderful!

And it's called *three ants were walking in the grass! And they were carrying a cheese puff on their heads!*

My heart got very thumping.

"NOODLE! HEY, NOODLE! I FOUND FRIENDS! AND THEY'VE BROUGHT A DELICIOUS CHEESE SNACK!"

After that, I picked up the ants and the cheese puff. And I dropped them right inside the jar.

And that is not the only good news!

Because just then, a big, buzzy fly landed right on my sweater sleeve! And I swatted him with the jar lid! And he did not even die that much!

I put him in the jar, too.

Then I danced and danced all over my yard.

Because now Noodle had friends!

And I had pets for Pet Day!

And that is called *happily ever after!*

# 6/ Sparkle

I runned into the house very thrilled.

"Mother! Mother! I found friends for Noodle! I found Buzzy the Swatted Fly! Plus also I found three ants and a cheese puff!"

Mother looked at the friends.

"Oh my," she said kind of soft.

"I know it, Mother! I know it is *oh my!* Noodle will *love* these guys! I know he will!"

After that, I quick took the jar to my

room. And I put it on my bed. And I waited for Noodle to meet his new friends.

I waited the whole entire afternoon.

Only Noodle never came out.

At dinnertime, I walked to the kitchen very slumping.

"Noodle is still hiding," I said. "Plus the ants ate the cheese puff. And Buzzy the Swatted Fly bit the dust."

Mother lifted me into my chair. She put stew on my plate.

"Yeah, only how can I even eat stew? 'Cause I am depressed, I tell you," I said.

Just then, someone opened the front door.

It was my Grandma Helen Miller.

She was bringing the ice chest back.

And guess what?

There was a giant fish in that thing!

My eyes popped out of my head!

"Grandma Miller! Grandma Miller! That fish is almost as big as me!" I said real thrilled.

Grandma Miller looked proud of herself.

"It's called a largemouth bass," she said. "He's a beaut, isn't he?"

"He *is*, Grandma! He is a beaut! Look at how shiny his skin is! Let's name him Sparkle! Want to? Huh, Grandma? Want to name him Sparkle?"

Grandma Miller laughed.

"Name him whatever you want, sweetie," she said. "We've got three more in the truck just like him. Come on, everybody. Come see them."

That's how come Mother and Daddy went out to the truck.

Only not me.

'Cause I wanted to stay with Sparkle, that's why!

I waved at that guy in the ice water.

"Hello, Sparkle. How are you today?" I said. "I am fine. Are you fine, too?"

I patted his head.

"Want to swim, Sparkle? Huh? Want to swim in the freezy water?"

After that, I got down on my knees. And I swimmed him all around.

"I wish you were my fish, Sparkle. If you were my fish, I would take you to school for Show and Tell. And you would be the star of the show."

Just then, I got goosebumps on my skin.

'Cause that was the bestest idea I ever heard of!

"Sparkle! Hey, Sparkle! Maybe you can come to Pet Day with me! 'Cause you are way better than my pet jar!"

After that, I lifted that big guy right out of the water.

Only too bad for me. 'Cause Sparkle fell on the floor.

"Oh dear," I said. "You are a chubby one, Sparkle. And so how will I even get you to school? That's what I would like to know."

Just then, I saw Tickle's dog leash.

It was hanging over the chair.

I danced all around the kitchen.

"A leash, Sparkle! A leash is the answer to our problem!"

After that, I quick grabbed the leash. And I put it over Sparkle's head. And I pulled him all around the floor!

He slided as easy as pie!

Just then, the back door opened.

"JUNIE B. JONES! WHAT IN THE WORLD DO YOU THINK YOU ARE DOING?"

It was Mother.

She was back from the truck, apparently.

"I think I am sliding Sparkle," I said kind of nervous. "We are practicing for Pet Day."

Mother shook her head real fast.

"Oh no. No way, missy. You are *not* taking that fish to Pet Day," she said.

"Yes, Mother! Yes way! I *have* to! I have to take Sparkle! I love this slippery guy! Please, Mother? Please? Please?"

Mother did some deep breathing.

Then she sat down next to me. And she made her voice not yell.

"Okay. I want you to listen to me very closely," she said. "I know you like this fish.

And I know you would like to take him to school for Pet Day. But Pet Day is for *live* pets, Junie B. And maybe you don't realize this...but the thing is, honey...Sparkle is *dead*."

I nodded my head.

"Not a problem," I said.

Mother did a frown.

"Not a problem? What do you *mean* 'not a problem'? Of course it's a problem. You can't take a dead fish to school."

I raised my eyebrows at her.

"How come? Is it in the rules?" I asked.

"No. Of course it's not in the rules," said Mother.

I smiled.

"Good. Then I can take him," I said.

After that, Mother stared at me a real long time.

Then she closed her eyes.

And she put her head on her place mat.

And she didn't eat her stew.

# 7/ Sneaky Grandma Miller

Grandma Miller stoled Sparkle!

She waited till I took my bath.

Then she sneaked into the kitchen.

And she took Sparkle home with her!

I runned all around in a tizzy.

"SHE STOLED HIM! GRANDMA MILLER STOLED SPARKLE! AND NOBODY EVEN STOPPED THAT WOMAN!"

Mother said to quiet my voice.

"Your grandmother did not *steal* Sparkle, Junie B. She caught him at the lake. That fish was hers, remember?"

She picked me up and carried me to bed.

"You're just going to have to accept this, Junie B." she said. "You cannot take a dead animal to school for Pet Day. End of story."

After that, she kissed me good night on my cheek.

And guess what?

I did not kiss back.

On Monday morning, Grampa Frank Miller babysitted me before school.

I did not speak to that guy.

'Cause he is married to the thief of Sparkle, that's why.

I ate my breakfast very silent.

Grampa Miller looked at my pet jar on the counter.

"Boy oh boy. Look at those ants, would you?" he said. "They're always on the go, aren't they?"

He squinted his eyes at them.

"What's that they're carrying around on their heads?"

I did a frown.

Then I thought very careful. 'Cause the cheese puff was already gone. And so what could they be carrying?

Just then, my eyes got big and wide.

'Cause I had a bad feeling about this situation, that's why.

I runned to my jar speedy fast.

"OH NO!" I hollered. "OH NO! OH NO! IT'S BUZZY THE SWATTED FLY!"

I quick took off the lid.

"PUT HIM DOWN! YOU PUT HIM DOWN RIGHT NOW! AND I *MEAN* IT!"

The ants did not obey me.

That's how come I zoomed them out to the grass. And I shaked them right out of my jar.

"GO HOME ANTS!" I hollered. "YOU GO HOME THIS VERY MINUTE!"

The ants went home.

I brushed my hands together very proud.

'Cause I saved Buzzy, that's why.

After that, I reached in the grass and picked up my jar. Only something did not feel right, exactly.

I looked inside of it.

Oh no!

It was empty!

All of the dirt was gone!

And Noodle was gone, too!

"NOODLE!" I shouted. "NOODLE! NOODLE! WHERE ARE YOU? WHERE ARE YOU?"

Then I crawled all over in the grass. And I searched and searched and searched.

But I never saw Noodle again.

# 8/
## A Surprise
## in the Freezer!

I cried on my bed for a real long time.

"Pet Day is ruined! It's ruined! It's ruined! It's ruined!"

Grampa Miller looked all over the house for pictures of Tickle.

He taped some on cardboard. And brought them to my room.

"Look," he said. "This doesn't look too bad, does it?"

I raised my sagging head off the pillow.

Then I looked at the pictures. And I patted him real gentle.

"You did your best, old man," I said very soft.

Grampa Miller rolled his eyes up at the ceiling. I looked up there, too. But I didn't see anything.

After that, I got out of bed. And I dressed myself for school. And I walked to the kitchen very slumping.

Grampa Miller made me a turkey sandwich.

"What do you want to drink?" he asked.

I did a sad sigh.

"Orange juice, please," I said.

Grampa Miller opened the refrigerator.

"Hmm...orange juice, orange juice...I don't see any orange juice," he said.

I went over and helped him look.

We couldn't find the orange juice anywhere. Not even in the freezer.

Just then, my grampa moved the frozen vegetables.

And guess what?

My heart almost stopped breathing!

'Cause I couldn't believe my eyeballs, that's why!

"GRAMPA MILLER! GRAMPA MILLER! DO YOU SEE WHAT I SEE? DO YOU, HUH? DO YOU? DO YOU?"

Grampa Miller looked closer.

"Well, I don't see any orange juice. That's for sure," he said.

I danced all around the room.

"NO, GRAMPA! NOT ORANGE JUICE! A PET! I SEE A PET FOR PET DAY! SEE IT, GRAMPA? SEE IT IN THERE?"

Then I clapped my hands real joyful!

And I skipped to the freezer!

And I grabbed it right off the shelf!

# 9/ My Proudest Honor

Pet Day in Room Nine was very exciting!

There were cages with furry animals. And bowls with fish. Plus also there was a snake. And a hermit crab. And a rooster.

"That rooster is *mine*," said that meanie Jim I hate. "He will peck your head off if I tell him to. He will peck it right into a nub."

I made a sick face. 'Cause a nub does not sound pleasant.

Just then, Lucille skipped over to me.

"Look, Junie B.! Look at my darling riding outfit! See my darling riding hat? And see my darling riding pants? And look, Junie B.! Here's a picture of my darling pony! And look at my darling riding boots! They are genuine rawhide cowhide!"

I smiled very admiring.

"You are a beaut, Lucille," I said.

Grace pulled on my arm.

"Junie B.! Junie B.! Come see Slicky! He's my goldfish, remember? I bought him a brand-new bowl! Come see it! Come see it!"

Just then, my teacher clapped her loud hands together.

"Boys and girls! Everyone needs to sit down right now! What an exciting day we're going to have in Room Nine today!"

We hurried up and sat.

Mrs. pointed to the pet table in the back of the room.

"Who would like to go first?" she asked. "Who would like to introduce us to their pet?"

"ME!" I shouted. "ME! ME! ME!"

Then I springed right out of my seat.

But Mrs. said *sit down* to me. And she called on Crybaby William. 'Cause that guy never springs, that's why.

William went to the pet table.

He pointed to his bullfrog named Wendell.

"I just got him on Saturday," said William very shy.

Mrs. smiled.

"Well, he certainly is a *handsome* bullfrog," she said. "Would you like to take Wendell out of his tank for us, William? Would you like to show the children how to hold a bullfrog?"

Then William's face got whitish and sick-
ish. And he started sweating a real lot.

That's how come Mrs. had to put a wet
towel on his head. And she said he didn't
have to hold Wendell.

Charlotte went next.

She showed us her bunny named Slippers.

She carried him all around the room.

And she let us pet his head.

Slippers smelled like stinky feet.

After Charlotte came Paulie Allen Puffer.

He showed us his parrot named Pirate Pete. Only too bad for Pirate Pete. 'Cause he kept on saying a bad word. And he wouldn't even stop. And so Mrs. had to send Pirate Pete to the office.

After that, lots of children showed pictures of their dogs and cats.

Plus Jamal Hall showed us his lizard named Gizzard.

And a boy named Ham showed us his hamster named Elvis.

Finally, I raised my hand real calm.

"It's nice to see you being so polite, Junie B. Would you like to go next?" Mrs. asked. "Did you bring a picture of your dog?"

I shook my head. "No," I said. "'Cause I didn't want to bring a picture, remember? I wanted to bring a real actual pet. Only too bad for me. 'Cause Mother said no raccoon. And then my Grandma Helen Miller stoled Sparkle. Plus also I lost my Noodle. And then we couldn't find the orange juice. And so that's how come my grampa moved the frozen vegetables. And boom! I saw a pet in there! So I put him in my backpack! And here he is now!"

After that, I quick unzipped my zipper pocket. And I held up my pet for everyone to see.

"FISH STICK!" I said real delighted. "I NAMED HIM FISH STICK BECAUSE HE'S A FISH STICK, OF COURSE!"

Room Nine stared and stared.

Then all of a sudden, everyone laughed at once.

"YOU GOONIE BIRD!" yelled that meanie Jim. "Fish sticks aren't pets! Fish sticks are *dinner!*"

I felt very shrinking inside.

"But...but fish sticks *have* to be pets. Right, Mrs.? Right?" I asked. "'Cause fish sticks are fish. Aren't they? And fish are pets. Right?"

Mrs. was hiding behind her hands. She peeked at me between her fingers.

"Um…yes. Sure. Of course fish are pets," she said.

I felt a teeny bit better.

"So then fish sticks can be pets, too. Right?" I said.

Mrs. hided a little while longer.

Then finally, she took a big breath. And she got up from her desk.

"Well, let's see. Maybe we should see what the dictionary has to say about this," she said.

After that, she took out her dictionary. And she looked up the word *pet*.

She read us what it said.

"*Pet*," she said. "*Any tamed animal that is kept as a companion.*"

"Okay," she said. "Now that we have

the definition, let's see if Fish Stick fits the bill."

She looked at me.

"Junie B., is Fish Stick tame? Or is he wild?"

"Tame," I said. "Fish Stick is very, *very* tame. He won't even peck your head into a nub."

"Okay, good," said Mrs. "And would you say that Fish Stick is a good *companion*, Junie B.? Can you take him lots of places? And does he behave himself pretty well?"

"Yes," I said. "Fish Stick can even go more places than my dog, probably. 'Cause I can put Fish Stick right in my backpack. And he doesn't even say a peep!"

Mrs. smiled real happy.

Then she walked to my table. And she shaked my hand.

"Well, then, congratulations," she said. "According to the dictionary, Fish Stick is *definitely* a pet."

After that, she took Fish Stick out of my hand. And she carried him to the pet table.

And guess what? She put him right next to Slicky!

"Grace! Hey, Grace! Now our fishes can be friends just like us!" I said real delighted.

Just then, I heard a croaking noise.

It came from Wendell the bullfrog, I think.

Then Wendell croaked even louder!

And that made Slicky the goldfish jump in his water!

And that made the rooster cock-a-doodle-doo!

And that made Slippers thump his loud foot!

And then his cage door accidentally came open. And he hopped right off the table!

"OH NO!" yelled Room Nine. "OH NO! OH NO!"

And then all of us chased Slippers all over the place. And he hopped and hopped until Mrs. caught him in the trash can.

It was the excitingest adventure Room Nine ever even had!

And that's not even the bestest part of Pet Day!

'Cause at the end of school, Mrs. gave out special ribbons to all the pets.

And the rooster got SCREECHIEST!

And Pirate Pete got TALKIEST!

And Slicky got BUBBLIEST!

And Slippers got MOST RASCALLY RABBIT!

And Fish Stick got **MOST WELL-BEHAVED!!!!**

I did a gasp at that wonderful thing.
Then I shaked and shaked Mrs.'s hand.
"Thank you, Mrs! Thank you, thank

Most Well-Behaved

you! 'Cause this is the proudest honor I ever imagined!"

Mrs. laughed.

She said me and Fish Stick made her day.

Then she gave me a hug.

And that is called a perfect ending!